At EEYORES GLOOMY PLACE

First published in Great Britain 2003
By Egmont Books Limited
239 Kensington High Street, London W8 6SA
Illustrated by Andrew Grey
Based on the 'Winnie-the-Pooh' works
By A.A. Milne and E.H. Shepard
© 2003 Disney Enterprises, Inc.
Designed by Clare Doughty
Edited by Catherine Shoolbred
Design © 2003 Egmont Books Limited
All Rights Reserved.

1 3 5 7 9 10 8 6 4 2

ISBN 1 4052 0527 X

Printed in Singapore.

Eeyore stood by the stream, and looked at himself in the water.

"Pathetic," he said. "That's what it is. Pathetic." He turned, splashed across the stream and turned to look at himself in the water again. "As I thought," he said. "No better from this side. But nobody cares." There was a crackling noise in the bracken, and out came Pooh.

"Good morning, Eeyore," said Pooh.

"Good morning, Pooh Bear," said Eeyore, gloomily. "If it is a good morning, which I doubt."

"Oh!" said Pooh and he sat down on a large stone and sang Cottleston Pie for Eeyore:

Cottleston, Cottleston, Cottleston Pie,
A fly can't bird, but a bird can fly.
Ask me a riddle and I reply:
"Cottleston, Cottleston, Cottleston Pie."

Cottleston, Cottleston, Cottleston Pie,
A fish can't whistle and neither can I.
Ask me a riddle and I reply:
"Cottleston, Cottleston, Cottleston Pie."

Cottleston, Cottleston, Cottleston Pie,
Why does a chicken, I don't know why.
Ask me a riddle and I reply:
"Cottleston, Cottleston, Cottleston Pie."

"That's right," said Eeyore. "Sing. Umty-tiddly, umpty-too. Enjoy yourself."

"I am," said Pooh. "But you seem so sad, Eeyore."

"Sad? Why should I be sad? It's my birthday. The happiest day of the year."

"Your birthday?" said Pooh, in great surprise.

"Of course it is. Can't you see? Look at all the presents I have had." He waved a foot from side to side.

Pooh looked – first to the right and then to the left.

"Presents?" said Pooh. "Where? I can't see them!"

"Neither can I," said Eeyore. "Joke," he explained. "Ha, ha!"

Pooh scratched his head being a little puzzled.

"But is it **really** your birthday?" he asked.

"It is."

"Oh! Well, **many happy returns** of the day, Eeyore."

"And many happy returns to you, Pooh Bear."

"But it isn't *my* birthday."

"No, it's mine."

"But you said 'Many happy returns' –"

"Well, why not? You don't want to be **miserable** on my birthday, do you?" said Eeyore. "It's bad enough being **miserable** myself, what with no presents and **no proper notice taken of me at all**, but if everybody else is going to be **miserable** too . . ."

This was **too much** for Pooh. "Stay there!" he called, as he hurried home; for he felt he must get Eeyore a **present** of some sort at once and he could always think of a proper one afterwards.

Outside his house, Pooh found Piglet jumping up and down trying to reach the knocker.

"What are you trying to do?" asked Pooh.

"I was trying to reach the knocker," said Piglet. "I just came round–"

"Let me do it for you," said Pooh, kindly.

So he reached up and knocked at the door.

"I have just seen Eeyore," he began, "poor Eeyore is very Gloomy because it's his birthday, and nobody has taken any notice of it, and what a long time whoever lives here is taking to answer this door."

"But Pooh," said Piglet, "it's your own house!"

"Oh!" said Pooh. "So it is. Well, let's go in."

So in they went.

The first thing Pooh did was to go to the cupboard to see if he had quite a small jar of honey left. And he had, so he took it down.

"I'm giving this to Eeyore," he explained, "as a **present**. What are you going to give?"

"Couldn't I give it too?" said Piglet. "From **both** of us?"

"No," said Pooh. "That would not be a **good plan**."

"All right, then, I'll give him a balloon. I've got one left from my party. I'll go and get it now, shall I?" said Piglet.

"That, Piglet, is a very good idea. It is just what Eeyore wants to cheer him up. Nobody can be uncheered with a balloon."

So off Piglet trotted, and in the other direction went Pooh, with his jar of honey.

Pooh hadn't gone more than half-way when a sort of
funny feeling began to creep all over him. It began
at the tip of his nose and trickled all through him and
out at the soles of his feet. It was just as if somebody
inside him were saying, 'Now then, Pooh, time for a
little something.'

So Pooh sat down to eat the honey.

As he took his last lick, he thought, "Now where was I going?" Then suddenly he remembered, he had eaten Eeyore's birthday present! Then he thought: "Well, it's a very nice pot, and if I washed it clean, and got somebody to write 'A Happy Birthday' on it, Eeyore could keep things in it, which might be Useful."

As Pooh was passing the Hundred Acre Wood, he went
to call on Owl, who lived there.

"Many happy returns of Eeyore's birthday," said Pooh.
"I'm giving Eeyore a **Useful Pot** to keep things in,
and I wanted to ask you–"
Owl looked at the pot. "You ought to write 'A Happy
Birthday' on it," he added.
"That was what I wanted to ask you," said Pooh.
"Because my spelling is Wobbly and the letters
get in the wrong places. Would you write
'A Happy Birthday' on it for me?"

"Can you read, Pooh?" Owl asked, a little anxiously. "There's a notice about knocking and ringing outside my door, which Christopher Robin wrote. Could you read it?"

"Christopher Robin told me what it said, and then I could," said Pooh.

"Well, I'll tell you what this says, and then you'll be able to," said Owl.

This is what Owl wrote:

HIPY PAPY BTHUTHDTH THUTHDA BTHUTHDY.

"I'm just saying 'A Happy Birthday'," said Owl, nervously.

"It's a nice long one," said Pooh, very much impressed by it.

"Well, actually, of course, I'm saying 'A very Happy Birthday with love from Pooh.'"

While all this was happening, Piglet had gone back to his house to get Eeyore's balloon. He held it **tightly** against himself so it shouldn't blow away, and ran as fast as he could to get to Eeyore before Pooh so he would be the first one to give a present. And running along, thinking how pleased Eeyore would be, he tripped on a rabbit hole, and fell flat on his face.

BANG!!!???!!!

Piglet wondered what had happened.
Had the Forest blown up?
Or had he and was he now alone on the moon
or somewhere?
Piglet got up.
He was still
in the
Forest!

"That's funny,"
he thought. "I
wonder what that bang was. And where's my
balloon? And what's that small piece of damp rag?"
It was the balloon!

"Oh, dear!" said Piglet. "Oh, dearie, dearie, dear!
I can't go back, and I haven't another balloon. Perhaps
Eeyore doesn't like balloons so very much."
So he trotted on, rather sadly now, and soon reached
Eeyore at the stream.

"Many happy returns of the day," said Piglet, having now got closer.

Eeyore stopped looking at himself in the stream, and turned to stare at Piglet.

"Just say that again," he said, as he balanced on three legs, bringing his fourth leg up to his ear. He pushed his ear forward with his hoof.

"Many happy returns of the day," said Piglet, again.

"My birthday?" said Eeyore.

"Yes, Eeyore, and I've brought you a present. A balloon."

"Balloon?" said Eeyore. "One of those big coloured things you blow up?"

"Yes, but I'm very sorry, Eeyore – I fell down."

"Dear, how unlucky! You didn't hurt yourself, Little Piglet?"

"No, but I – I – oh, Eeyore, I burst the balloon!"

There was a very long silence.

"My balloon?" said Eeyore at last.

Piglet nodded. "Yes, Eeyore," said Piglet, sniffing a little. "Here it is. With – with many happy returns of the day."

And he gave Eeyore the small piece of damp rag.

"Is this it?" said Eeyore, a little surprised. "My present?"
Piglet nodded again.

"Thank you, Piglet," said Eeyore. "What colour was it when it – when it was a balloon?"

"Red."

"My favourite colour," said Eeyore, thoughtfully.
"Well, well."

Piglet felt very miserable, and didn't know what to say.

Suddenly, there was Pooh.

"Many happy returns of the day," said Pooh.

"Thank you, Pooh, I'm having them," said Eeyore, gloomily.

"I've brought you a little present," said Pooh, excitedly.

"It's a Useful Pot," said Pooh. "And it's got 'A Very Happy Birthday with love from Pooh' written on it. And it's for putting things in. There!"

When Eeyore saw the pot, he was quite excited.
"I believe my Balloon will go into that Pot!"
"Oh, no, Eeyore," said Pooh. "Balloons are much too
big to go into Pots."
"Not mine," said Eeyore proudly. "Look, Piglet!" And
as Piglet looked sadly round, Eeyore placed the balloon
carefully in the pot.
"So it does!" said Pooh. "It goes in!"
"So it does!" said Piglet. "And it comes out!"
"Doesn't it?" said Eeyore. "It goes in and
out like anything."

"I'm very glad," said Pooh, "that I thought of giving you a **Useful Pot** to put things in."

"I'm very glad," said Piglet, "that I thought of giving you **Something** to put in a Useful Pot."

But Eeyore wasn't listening. He was taking the balloon out, and putting it back again, as **happy** as could be.

 THIS STORY TOOK PLACE